Hello, Family Members,

O9-AID-593

Learning to read is one of the most important accomplishments of early childhood. **Hello Reader!** books are designed to help children become skilled readers who like to read. Beginning readers learn to read by remembering frequently used words like "the," "is," and "and"; by using phonics skills to decode new words; and by interpreting picture and text clues. These books provide both the stories children enjoy and the structure they need to read fluently and independently. Here are suggestions for helping your child *before*, *during*, and *after* reading:

Before
- Look at the cover and pictures and have your child predict what the story is about.
- Read the story to your child.
- Encourage your child to chime in with familiar words and phrases.
- Echo read with your child by reading a line first and having your child read it after you do.

During
- Have your child think about a word he or she does not recognize right away. Provide hints such as "Let's see if we know the sounds" and "Have we read other words like this one?"
- Encourage your child to use phonics skills to sound out new words.
- Provide the word for your child when more assistance is needed so that he or she does not struggle and the experience of reading with you is a positive one.
- Encourage your child to have fun by reading with a lot of expression . . . like an actor!

After
- Have your child keep lists of interesting and favorite words.
- Encourage your child to read the books over and over again. Have him or her read to brothers, sisters, grandparents, and even teddy bears. Repeated readings develop confidence in young readers.
- Talk about the stories. Ask and answer questions. Share ideas about the funniest and most interesting characters and events in the stories.

I do hope that you and your child enjoy this book.

— Francie Alexander
  Reading Specialist,
  Scholastic's Learning Ventures

Library of Congress Cataloging-in-Publication Data

Gave, Marc.
    Monkey see, monkey do / by Marc Gave; illustrated by Jacqueline Rogers.
       p.   cm. — (Hello reader)
    Summary: Rhyming text relates the antics of monkeys that play all day.
    ISBN 0-590-45801-9
    [1. Monkeys — Fiction. 2. Play — Fiction. 3. Stories in rhyme.]
    I. Rogers, Jacqueline, ill. II. Title. III. Series.
PZ8.3.G22Mo 1993
[E] — dc20
                                        91-45443
                                            CIP
                                          AC

42 41 40
                                         2 3 4 5 6 7/0

Printed in the U.S.A.

First Scholastic printing, January 1993

Monkey See, Monkey Do

by Marc Gave
Illustrated by Jacqueline Rogers

Hello Reader! — Level 1

SCHOLASTIC INC.
Cartwheel
·B·O·O·K·S·®

New York   Toronto   London   Auckland   Sydney
Mexico City   New Delhi   Hong Kong

Monkey me.
Monkey you.

Monkey see.
Monkey do.

Monkey on the left.

Monkey on the right.

Monkey in the middle.

Monkey out of sight.

Monkey up a tree.
Monkey on the ground.

Monkeys in a bunch, monkeying around.

Monkeys stay.

Monkeys stay.

Monkeys go.

Monkeys go fast.

Monkeys go slow.

Monkeys walk.

Monkeys run.

Monkeys have some monkey fun.

Monkeys bend.

Monkeys reach.

Monkeys lie
along the beach.

Monkeys swim.
Monkeys row.

Monkeys swing
to and fro.

Monkeys play
while the sky is light.

Monkeys sleep through the night.

Good night.